Much Ado About Nothing

Written by William Shakespeare

Retold by Sue Purkiss

Illustrated by Amerigo Pinelli

Collins

Characters

Don Pedro, a prince – his father is the king of Sicily

Benedick, a friend and follower of Don Pedro

Claudio, a friend and follower of Don Pedro

Don John, half-brother of Don Pedro

Borachio and **Conrad**, followers of Don John

Leonato, governor of Messina

Hero, Leonato's daughter

Beatrice, Leonato's orphaned niece

Antonio, Leonato's brother

Margaret and **Ursula**, Hero's attendants

Friar Francis

Dogberry, in charge of the Watch

1 The prince comes to town!

Beatrice pushed open her window and leant out, smiling. It was such a lovely morning!

Then she noticed a small cloud of dust on the road that led to her uncle's house. Excited, she called out to her cousin, "Hero, wake up, you lazybones! Someone's coming!"

In no time at all, she and Hero were dressed and running out into the courtyard. Hero's father, Leonato, was already there with his brother, Antonio, who was visiting them. They both looked very pleased.

"Girls, girls!" said Leonato. "A message from the prince, Don Pedro – he's on his way to see us. Isn't that marvellous? He's been fighting on the other side of the island."

"Oh yes," said Beatrice, tossing her head. "And I suppose that talkative friend of his, Benedick, will be with him?"

Leonato wagged his finger at her. "No doubt, no doubt. And you must see if you can manage to be polite to him!"

"Of course," said Beatrice sweetly.

Soon, the house was a whirl of activity. Windows were flung open, beds were made, and delicious smells drifted out of the kitchen. By the time the prince and his men galloped in, Leonato and his household were ready.

"Don't they look handsome in their uniforms?" whispered Hero. She was quite a bit younger than Beatrice, and a little shy – she'd never seen the prince before. "Who's who?"

"Well, the one in the middle is the prince," murmured Beatrice. "The one beside him – the nice-looking one – is Claudio. The one with the silly grin – that's Benedick. He comes from Padua, and I don't know why he didn't stay there. And the miserable one, that's Don Pedro's brother, Don John. They don't get on. They say it's because Don John is jealous – Don Pedro is the oldest, so he'll be king one day. And he's much nicer too, so everyone likes him better, and Don John just can't bear it."

They both curtseyed deeply to the prince. Then, as Hero glanced up through her eyelashes, she saw that Claudio was gazing at her. She looked away, feeling shy, but she could still feel his eyes on her, and she smoothed her hair and wished she'd put her best dress on.

Beatrice and Benedick were already arguing.

"How've you been, since I saw you last?" he asked her. "I expect you've missed me terribly."

"Oh yes," she said. "Like a bad cold."

"Actually, you look rather as if you have a cold. Your eyes are quite watery. Or are those tears of joy at seeing me again?"

"More like tears of sorrow," she replied. "It's been so delightfully peaceful since I last saw you."

"Ahem!" said Leonato, interrupting them. "Welcome, everyone, and – er – Don John. I hope you'll spend some time with us?"

"Oh, at least a month, I should think," said Don Pedro cheerily. "We're ready for a rest."

"Marvellous! Come inside. We're going to have a masked ball this evening – what do you say to that, eh?"

2 Love at first sight

As Leonato led the others indoors, Claudio hung back with Benedick.

"Come for a walk," he hissed. "I want to talk to you!" As they walked down a path lined with orange trees, he demanded: "Did you see that girl? Isn't she the loveliest thing you've ever laid eyes on?"

"What? Who?"

"Hero, of course!"

"Oh. Well, she's all right, I suppose. Not a patch on her cousin. Though she's probably got a sweeter temper."

"Why, she's as far above Beatrice as – as the sun is above the earth! Benedick, I'm in love!"

As he was speaking, the prince came along another path, looking for his friends. He'd heard what Claudio had said. "That's a bit sudden!" he said.

"Madness!" declared Benedick. "Love, marriage – it's all nonsense."

Don Pedro smiled. "Oh, come, Benedick, we're not all like you – and not all girls are like Beatrice!"

"Fine," said Benedick, holding up his hands. "I'll leave you to it." And he strolled off, pulling an orange from a tree and cutting it in half with his knife.

"I know it's sudden," said Claudio seriously. "But it's true. I want to marry her."

"It'd be a good match," mused Don Pedro. "She inherits everything. Well – if you're really, really sure ...?"

"I've never been so certain of anything in my life!" declared Claudio.

"Then – tonight, I'll speak to her for you. And if she consents, I'll speak to Leonato. How does that sound?"

Claudio smiled happily. "It sounds absolutely marvellous!"

Antonio had no children of his own, but he was very fond of Hero, his niece. So when his servant hurried up to him and told him about a conversation he'd overheard in the garden – concerning Hero and Don Pedro – his eyes lit up.

"Oh my goodness! The prince – and our little Hero! Well, this is marvellous news! I must go and tell my brother – at once!"

Leonato could hardly believe it. "The prince wants to marry Hero? I could never have imagined such a splendid match! Are you sure?"

"Oh yes – my man heard it quite plainly. He's going to speak to her tonight."

"Then I must warn her – she must prepare herself. Oh, this is so exciting ..."

Meanwhile, Don John had found a quiet part of the garden and was sitting moodily on a bench with his servant, Conrad. All around him were sweet-smelling roses, and the sea sparkled in the distance, but Don John saw none of this. All he could think about was how miserable he was.

"If only I'd been born first," he complained. "Then I'd be my father's heir, and they'd all look up to me. Instead, all I get is the leftovers – no respect, no riches, no nothing. It's no wonder I don't go round with a smile on my face all the time, like those idiots who follow my brother."

"They certainly are annoying, my lord," said Conrad sympathetically. "Especially that Claudio."

"Yes, he's the worst. I don't understand what my brother sees in him."

Just then, his other servant, Borachio, came along the path.

Don John stared at him. "Why are you looking so pleased with yourself?"

"Because," said Borachio, "I just happened to hear a conversation. Between your brother and Claudio. And guess what? That silly fool Claudio has all of a sudden fallen in love with Hero, the old man's daughter. And so your brother is going to speak to her tonight, and if she agrees, he'll ask Leonato if she can marry Claudio."

"And you think that's a good thing?" scowled Don John.

"Oh yes," smiled Borachio. "Because I know how we can stir things up a bit. Trust me, my lord – this marriage won't take place. And your brother and Claudio are going to look very silly indeed ..."

3 The ball

A great silver moon hung high in the sky, while down in the garden, strings of lanterns glittered in the trees. Guests strolled along the many paths, enjoying the sound of the fountains and the perfume of the flowers, while musicians sang and played their lutes. It was to be a masked ball, so everyone was looking forward to an evening of fun and surprises – because with faces hidden behind masks, how could you tell who your partner was?

Leonato and Antonio were waiting with the two girls, Hero and Beatrice, to welcome the chief guests – the prince and his party. The talk had turned, strangely enough, to love and marriage.

"Come now, Beatrice," teased Leonato. "Are you quite sure you don't have a soft spot for Benedick?"

"Yes," put in his brother, Antonio. "To say you don't like him, you seem to spend an awful lot of time talking to him – or about him!"

Beatrice smiled sweetly. "Oh, I'll exchange a few insults with him now and again," she said. "It passes the time and it amuses me. But don't talk to me about love, and certainly not about marriage. I'm simply not interested. No," she declared, "I'll never marry. I'm far too sensible. Hero, on the other hand ..."

It's quite different for Hero," said Leonato, smiling at his daughter fondly. "She'll inherit my estate when I'm gone, so she must find someone to help her run it. Unlike you, my dear niece, she has obligations. And I know you won't let me down, will you, my dear?"

"Of course not, Father," said Hero warmly. "If the prince does ask me to marry him – then I know my duty. Oh, look – here they come! Quickly, we must put on our masks!"

But Beatrice had been watching her closely. Her cousin had looked sad. And when the prince and his men arrived, it wasn't Don Pedro on whom her eyes rested – it was Claudio.

17

Soon the dancing began. Beatrice found herself partnering Benedick – she recognised the mocking blue eyes she could see through the eyeholes in his mask.

"Won't you tell me who you are?" she teased. "I really don't know."

"Couldn't possibly," he said. "Not unless you say first. I don't mind who you are provided you're not Beatrice."

"What's wrong with Beatrice?" she said. "I mean – they say she's very nice. And clever. And funny!"

He burst out laughing, and swirled her round. "Well, they've certainly got that wrong!"

Meanwhile, Don Pedro had drawn Hero aside, and was speaking softly to her – while in another part of the garden, Don John and Borachio were searching for Claudio. When they found him, they pretended to think he was Benedick.

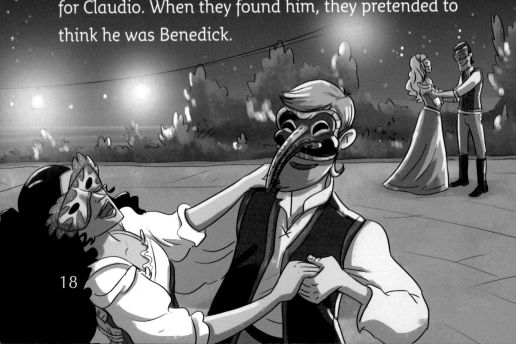

"Ah, Signor Benedick, I think?"

"Perhaps," murmured Claudio, wondering what the prince's unpleasant brother was up to now. "Can I help you, sirs?"

"I hope so." Don John looked round, and lowered his voice. "My brother's suspicious of me. I'm afraid he only keeps me with him because he doesn't trust me. But I know he'll listen to you. And I just overheard something which could cause him great harm. He's asked Hero to marry him!"

"What?" spluttered Claudio.

"Yes," said Don John smoothly. "Difficult to believe he could be so stupid, isn't it? She's far below him in rank – it would be a dreadful match for him. Anyway, I thought, you being his friend, you could have a word ... Oh, someone's coming – I can leave it with you?"

And he and Borachio melted away into the darkness.
Claudio slumped down on to a bench, tore off his mask
and buried his face in his hands.

"What's up with you?" said Benedick cheerfully.
"Love's young dream gone sour already?"

"Yes, it has!" said Claudio. When he told Benedick
what Don John had said, Benedick burst out laughing.

"Oh, don't be such a twit. Surely you don't
believe that!" he said.

"It's all very well for you," snapped Claudio. "You don't
know what love is! My life's ruined!"

He flounced off. Benedick sighed, and went off to find
the prince. Along the way, he bumped into Beatrice and
told her what had happened.

"Right," she said. "You find Hero and the prince, and
I'll get Claudio. How could he be so silly?"

Soon, it was all sorted out – Hero was overjoyed, the prince was amused and Claudio was embarrassed. Then they all trooped off to find Leonato, who was rather puzzled.

"So it's Claudio who wants to marry my daughter – not you, my lord?" he said.

"Yes," said the prince firmly. "Claudio. My dear friend, and a fine young man of excellent family."

"And they love each other," put in Beatrice.

"Oh. Yes. Splendid. Well then! It looks as if we're going to have a wedding! Hurrah!"

"Hurrah!" said Claudio, gazing fondly at Hero. "Could it be tomorrow?"

"Certainly not!" said Leonato. "These things take time. At least a few days ..."

21

4 Plots and plans

The next day, Don John was even unhappier than usual. He was almost snarling as he prowled up and down inside his room.

"Well, that went well, didn't it? Claudio and Hero are as happy as two little songbirds – yuck! And my brother is so pleased with himself it's quite sickening! Oh, he thinks he's so clever ... so much for you two and your brilliant ideas," he said, scowling at Conrad and Borachio.

"Patience, my lord, patience," said Borachio. "It's not over yet. You see, I know Margaret, Hero's maid. In fact," he smirked, "she's taken quite a fancy to me." Conrad snorted, and Borachio glared at him. "She has! And here's the thing. I've arranged to see her tonight. She's the same build as Hero, and her hair's the same colour – from the back, at nighttime, you wouldn't know the difference. Well, we'll fix it so Claudio and Don Pedro are outside Hero's window. They'll look up, and what will they see? They'll see Hero with another man!"

Don John's face lit up. "They'll be furious! Claudio won't question it – he was ready enough to believe ill even of the prince yesterday, wasn't he? Oh yes, he'll fall for it." He smiled, and put an arm round Borachio's shoulders. "You've done a good job, my friend, and you'll be well paid for your troubles. Oh, I can't wait to see Claudio's stupid face ..."

23

Unaware of Don John's plotting, Don Pedro was making some plans of his own. He, Claudio, Hero and Leonato were enjoying a glass of delicious orange juice from Leonato's own trees in a pleasant corner of the garden. "I've been thinking," he said, "about how we can amuse ourselves while we're waiting for the wedding. What do you say to us having a bit of fun with Beatrice and Benedick?"

"Oh yes!" said Claudio. "Great idea! Er – how do you mean?"

"Well – we make Benedick think that Beatrice is in love with him, and we make Beatrice think that Benedick is in love with her. See?"

Claudio still looked puzzled, but Leonato stroked his beard and smiled, and Hero clapped her hands in delight.

"And then we just stand back and watch the fun!" she said.

Don Pedro nodded. "Exactly!"

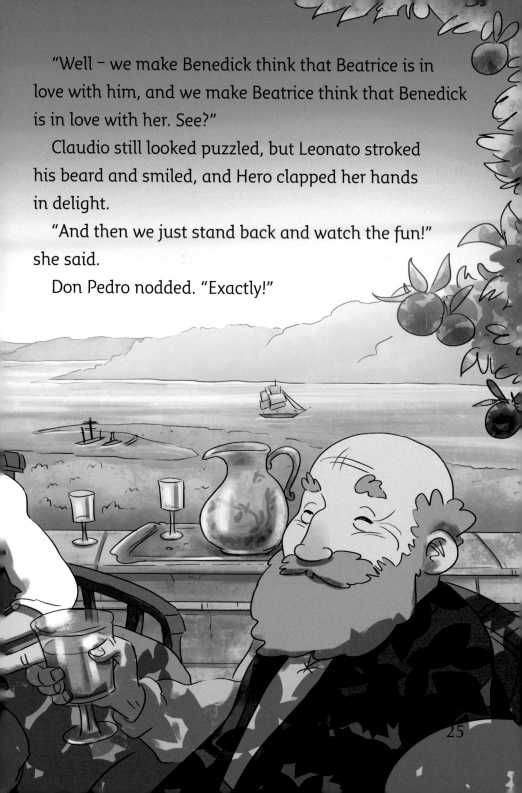

So it was that half an hour later, Don Pedro, Claudio and Leonato had found where Benedick was sitting in another part of the garden, writing in his notebook. (He fancied himself as a poet.) Pretending they hadn't seen him, they strolled along a nearby path.

"Really?" said Don Pedro. "Beatrice is in love with Benedick? But they can't stand each other!"

"Oh no," said Claudio. "It's absolutely true. She told Hero, and Hero told me. But she won't tell Benedick, because she thinks he'd just laugh at her. Shame, isn't it?"

And they walked on, trying not to laugh, as Benedick sat with his mouth open in astonishment.

Meanwhile, Hero was picking peaches in the orchard with her maids, Margaret and Ursula – all of them pretending not to see Beatrice, who was sitting under a tree eating an apple.

"No!" said Ursula. "Benedick in love with Beatrice? Surely not! Why, they do nothing but snap each other's heads off!"

Hero nodded. "It's true. Benedick told Claudio, and Claudio told me. But he won't tell Beatrice, because he thinks she'd just laugh at him."

There was a thwack as Beatrice's apple fell to the ground ...

5 Dark deeds

Benedick paced up and down in his room. His notebook lay open on his desk, and he was muttering to himself. "She's as lovely as ... a spoonful of sugar? No, too sweet ... the summer sun? No, too hot." Then he caught sight of himself in a mirror, tilted his head up and tried out a dashing smile.

"Why, my old friend – anyone would think you were in love!" teased Don Pedro, who'd been spying on him from the doorway with Claudio and Leonato.

"Eh? What nonsense. Don't be so ridiculous! Um – but Signor Leonato – a word, if you please."

He drew the old man into the room, shutting the door firmly on Don Pedro and Claudio, who had to smother their laughter.

But Don Pedro's face darkened as he saw his brother coming down the hall to speak to him.

"Brother – a word with you," said Don John. "With both of you. I've some bad news. In fact, I hardly know how to tell you – "

Minutes later, Claudio was white as a sheet, and Don Pedro looked furious.

"I simply can't believe that Hero would see someone else when she's engaged to Claudio. If this is more of your troublemaking – !"

Don John sighed and spread his arms out. "All you have to do is come with me tonight. Your own eyes will tell you that I speak only the truth – much as it pains me."

"If it's true," said the prince, "then the wedding must be cancelled."

Then Claudio spoke for the first time. "No," he said, tears rolling down his face. "If it's true, I'll wait till we're in the church. And there, I'll tell the whole world what Hero – my sweet Hero! – is really like."

That night, the local police force, the Watch, were lined up in front of their commander, Dogberry. "Now then, lads," he said, prowling up and down in front of them. "It's going to be a busy night for us, what with this wedding and all. All sorts of strangers in town – see? So keep your eyes peeled and your wits about you – if you've got any. Wits, that is." He stopped and glared at them. They shuffled their feet. "That was a joke, that was! Oh dearie me – why do I bother? Go on, off you go! And KEEP WATCH!"

Later that night, as the Watch were doing as they'd been told and looking out for suspicious characters, they came across Conrad and Borachio, who were slapping each other on the back and laughing.

"You should've seen Don Pedro's face when he saw you with Margaret at Hero's window!" said Conrad. "Fell for it hook, line and sinker! Mind you, it did look like Hero – brilliant job."

"I know! I could see, even from upstairs. And Claudio – honest, I thought he was going to burst into tears!"

The watchmen listened. They glanced at each other. "This don't sound right," whispered one.

"They was talking about the prince," muttered another.

"And Miss Hero – her who's getting married," said someone else.

"I say we should arrest them," said a third. "Let's go and tell Mr Dogberry."

So Borachio and Conrad were arrested and taken off to the cells.

The next morning, Dogberry and his deputy, Verges, went to see Leonato. But Leonato was impatient – it was the day of the wedding and there was a lot to do.

"What is it, Dogberry? Come on then – out with it!"

"Ah, well, you see, sir, it's like this. Last night, as my men were proceeding in an orderly fashion, keeping their wits about them, as I'd told them to do – "

"Yes, yes – what?"

"Eh? Oh, well – at the bottom of the hill, where there's that fountain that doesn't work properly any more – "

"Oh, I haven't got time for this – don't you understand? It's my daughter's wedding! Tell me about it later." And he hurried off, leaving Dogberry and Verges standing.

6 Disaster!

The way from Leonato's house to the church was lined with well-wishers. Hero ran along in a white dress, with ribbons and flowers in her hair, with Beatrice, Margaret and Ursula following. She couldn't wait to get to the church; this was going to be the happiest day of her life!

She ducked underneath the arch of flowers at the gate and hugged her father at the door. He held her at arms' length and gazed at her fondly.

"You look lovely, my dear," he said. "Now – are you ready? Then let's go in."

Musicians played as they walked up the aisle.
Friar Francis stood waiting – and there was Claudio with
his back to her, straight and tall. When she was beside
him, she glanced up at him shyly. But he didn't turn to
look at her, and his face looked white and very serious.
She felt a little chill – was he regretting his choice?
Surely not – he'd told her so many times how much he
loved her.

The service began. Soon, Father Francis asked Claudio: "Will you, Claudio, take Hero to be your lawful wedded wife?"

A smile trembled on Hero's lips. She felt as if she'd burst with happiness. But – what was Claudio saying?

"No! I won't! Look at her – she looks so sweet! But last night, I saw her – in the arms of another man!"

Hero gasped and clutched at his arm. "What are you saying? It's not true – it's not true!"

But he pushed her away – so hard that she stumbled and fell. There was a pain in her head – everything was going dark. She closed her eyes and fainted.

There was a terrible commotion. Beatrice rushed to Hero's side; everyone was talking at once.

"How dare you say such things about my daughter?" shouted Leonato.

"Because they're true! I saw her with my own eyes!"

"And so did I," said the prince. He put his hand on Leonato's shoulder. "I'm sorry, old friend. But it's true."

Leonato suddenly looked ten years older. "If it's true," he said, "then Hero's no daughter of mine. She's brought shame to our family."

"And to me!" shouted Claudio. "And to me!"

At that, Don Pedro led him away.

"Oh, for heaven's sake!" snapped Beatrice, glaring at Leonato. "Surely you can't believe this – this nonsense?"

"You heard the prince," he said sadly.

Friar Francis shook his head. "I was watching her the whole time," he said. "She was telling the truth. I'm certain of it. She's not guilty."

Leonato looked at him. "You think so? Truly?"

"Yes, I do," said Friar Francis. "May I make a suggestion? Tell everyone that Hero is dead. And then, while she's hidden away, we'll prove her innocence."

Benedick came forwards and touched Beatrice on the arm. "Come," he said gently, "let's carry your cousin home. Don't worry – everything's going to be all right. I promise."

39

Later, when Hero was in bed, Benedick and Beatrice found themselves alone together.

"You've been kind," she said. "Thank you."

Softly, he said, "Beatrice – I'd do anything for you. I love you."

She gazed at him. "Do you know – I believe I love you too! But is that true? Would you really do anything for me?"

He took her hand. "Yes," he said. "Anything."

She leant forward. "Then kill Claudio for me!"

He jumped. "I can't do that!"

"But you said – "

"And I meant it! But not that."

"So you care more for Claudio than you do for me!" she said angrily. "Don't you see how badly he's behaved, how cruel he's been?"

Benedick looked uncomfortable. "Yes, I do, but – " He thought for a moment. Then he took her hands and gazed into her eyes. "You're right. But I'm not just going to attack him like a coward. I'll challenge him to a duel. Will that do?"

She smiled through her tears, and nodded. "Yes," she said, "that'll certainly do."

41

7 Truth will out

The magistrate listened to Dogberry and Verges, hardly able to believe what he was hearing. Then he listened to Conrad and Borachio.

"So you – what's your name again? Borachio? You admit it?" he spluttered. "Don John, the prince's own brother, paid you to blacken the name of the Lady Hero? And Claudio believed you, and said he was going to accuse her at their wedding?"

"Exactly, sir! That's just what my lads heard them saying! This one was telling the other one all about it!" said Dogberry. "I never heard of such a thing. I've seen a lot in my time, but I'm not afraid to say – "

The magistrate nodded impatiently. He was really getting quite tired of the sound of Dogberry's voice.

"Yes, yes," he said, turning to Conrad and Borachio. "Well, you got what you wanted. Claudio did indeed accuse the Lady Hero. And the shock's killed her – yes, she's dead! What's more, I sent a messenger to call your master here – and he's disappeared. He's left you to it!"

Borachio groaned.

"Well, we must go to Leonato and tell him what's happened. Dogberry, Verges – bring the prisoners. They must explain themselves, both to the prince and Leonato."

Antonio had persuaded Leonato to take a walk. "A little fresh air will do you good, Brother," he said.

Leonato shook his head wearily. "Nothing will do me good," he said. "Not until my daughter's name is cleared, and Don Pedro and Claudio admit they were mistaken."

"Oh," said Antonio. "Well – here they come!"

"Good," said Leonato. He grabbed Claudio's arm. "You, sir! Aren't you ashamed of yourself?"

Claudio tried to pull away. "I only spoke the truth! I saw what I saw!"

"It's true," said Don Pedro gently. "I'm afraid there's no doubt, sir. I saw it too – Hero, in her room, with another man."

"No!" shouted Leonato.

"Yes!" shouted Claudio in return, putting his hand on his sword.

"Oh, kill someone else, would you? Well, that's all right! I'll fight you any time you choose!"

"And me, and me!" shouted Antonio. "You young villain!"

Don Pedro stood between them. "No," he said firmly. "Enough. Leonato, I feel very sorry for you. But Claudio speaks the truth, as I've said. Go home now."

"Scared of a fight, are you?" said Antonio, still furious.

But Leonato took his arm. "Come, Brother, come. This isn't over yet."

As they stumbled sadly away, Benedick came up to the prince and Claudio.

"Did you see that pair of greybeards?" joked Don Pedro. "They threatened us with a fight – can you believe it?"

"Why did they do that?" said Benedick quietly.

"Oh, they've some idea that we made a mistake – that somehow we didn't see Hero with another man."

"I think that too," said Benedick. "Because of you, an innocent girl's dead. And so, Claudio, I must challenge you to a duel."

Surprised, Claudio smiled. "Oh, very funny!"

Don Pedro looked amused too. "It's because he's in love. It's made him go crazy!"

Benedick's face was very serious. "I do love Beatrice, it's true. But the reason I'm going to fight you is because you've destroyed a sweet, innocent girl. Your brother, my lord, has run away. Perhaps you should think about that. Claudio – I'll expect to hear from you."

"Well!" said Claudio, staring after Benedick. "Who'd have thought it?"

"And who's this coming now?" said Don Pedro. "Why – those are my brother's men – in handcuffs! What can this mean?"

8 Celebrations!

Dogberry and Verges began to tell their tale – in great detail.

Impatiently, Borachio interrupted. "Enough, enough. I want to confess. Because of me and my master, the Lady Hero's dead. I never meant for that to happen – I never thought ... Well, it's too late now. But at least you should know the truth. Don John paid me to visit Margaret in Hero's rooms, and make it look as if she was Hero – I should say that Margaret had no idea of what I was up to. His job was to make sure that you, my lord, and Claudio, were watching. It all worked far too well. I'm more sorry than I can say – and I'll take my punishment willingly."

"Innocent," whispered Leonato. "I knew she was innocent!"

Don Pedro had turned white, and Claudio had fallen to his knees. Tears were running down his face. "What've I done? Hero – Hero!" He looked up at Leonato, and said in a broken voice, "Is there anything I can do to make up for it?"

Leonato looked at him. "Yes," he said. "Yes, there is. First, you must make the truth known – you must clear my daughter's name. And second – it just so happens that I have a niece, a girl you don't know, who lives nearby. She's very like Hero. You can't be my son-in-law now, but if you marry my niece, you'll at least be my nephew. Is it agreed?" he said gently.

"Whatever you say, sir, of course," said Claudio, looking a little sad.

"Then come to my house tomorrow, and Friar Francis shall marry you."

So the next morning, all those in Leonato's household gathered together, brimming with excitement. Hero couldn't wait to see Claudio's face when he realised she was alive after all. Privately, Beatrice thought she was a little too forgiving. And Benedick was relieved he wouldn't have to fight Claudio after all.

"I think he should be ashamed of himself!" she whispered to Benedick. "I certainly wouldn't marry him."

"I should think not," said Benedick. "After all, you're marrying me."

She looked at him. "Marrying you? Who said I was marrying you?"

"Oh! But I thought – "

"Oh, you thought, did you? Well, perhaps you'd better think again!"

"Now look, Beatrice – "

But she burst into laughter, and he realised that, as usual, she was only joking. Just then, there was a commotion at the door.

"They're here! Quick – my veil!" said Hero.

Beatrice helped Hero to cover her face, and they all looked suitably serious. Leonato led Claudio over to Hero. "Here's my niece, Claudio."

"Oh! Well then – won't you put back your veil, so that I can see your face?"

"Certainly not!" said Leonato firmly. "Not till you're well and truly married."

"Then give me your hand," said Claudio, "in front of Friar Francis here, and I'll swear that if you wish it, I'll be your husband."

At that, Hero flung back her veil. "See – it's me!"

"What? But how – who – what? I don't understand!"

And then there were lots of explanations, and lots of laughter, and quite a few tears.

"I can't believe it," said Claudio, wiping his eyes, unable to stop smiling. "And I definitely don't deserve it. But I'm so relieved it's you, and not this mystery cousin!"

"Well, just so long as you trust me from now on," Hero managed, before Claudio flung his arms around her.

Beatrice and Benedick decided that, since Friar Francis and all their friends were already there, they might as well get married too. (Some people were more surprised by that than by Hero being alive after all.) And then there was music, and dancing and a delicious wedding cake.

In the middle of all that, a messenger came to say that Don John had been captured.

"Oh, never mind him," said the prince. "We'll decide what to do about him tomorrow. In the meantime – let's enjoy ourselves!"

Benedick took Beatrice's hands, to draw her into the dance. "Are you happy?" he asked.

She smiled at him. "My mother used to say that a star danced when I was born, and so I'd always be happy. And do you know? I think she was right!"

Much Ado About Nothing

55

Ideas for reading

Written by Clare Dowdall, PhD
Lecturer and Primary Literacy Consultant

Reading objectives:
- check that the book makes sense to them, discussing their understanding and exploring the meaning of words in context
- draw inferences such as inferring characters' feelings, thoughts and motives from their actions, and justify inferences with evidence
- discuss and evaluate how authors use language, including figurative language, considering the impact on the reader

Spoken language objectives:
- participate in discussions, presentations, performances, role play, improvisations and debates

Curriculum links: PSHE – healthy relationships

Resources: art materials for making masks; paper plates

Build a context for reading
- Read children the title *Much Ado About Nothing*. Ask them to suggest what it might mean.
- Read the blurb aloud, and ask children if it helps them to understand that it means a lot of fuss about nothing.
- Ask children what they think might happen in this famous comedy by William Shakespeare.

Understand and apply reading strategies
- Turn to pp2–3. Work together to sketch a web to show how the characters in the story relate to each other.
- Walk through Chapter 1 together to get a sense of the plot and characters. Then cast children as characters and a narrator and read the chapter aloud together, working on expressive and fluent reading.